FALLING FOR CHRISTMAS

AMY L. GALE

5 PRINCE PUBLISHING

Published by 5 PRINCE PUBLISHING & BOOKS, LLC

PO Box 865, Arvada, CO 80001

www.5PrinceBooks.com

ISBN digital: 978-1-63112-326-9

ISBN print: 978-1-63112-327-6

Cover Credit: Marianne Nowicki

4272023

THIS TITLE WAS PREVIOUSLY PUBLISHED IN THE 2022 A ROMANCE TO REMEMBER ANTHOLOGY BY 5 PRINCE PUBLISHING

ALSO BY AMY L. GALE

Blissful Disaster

Blissful Tragedy

Christmas Blitz

FALLING FOR CHRISTMAS

.

CHAPTER 1

NEWBIE

"THERE'S NO WAY I'M LETTING HIM GET AWAY WITH THIS." I STOMP forward, rock salt crackles under my boots with each step.

"I'm with you, Nat," my best friend Belle says as she navigates the sidewalk, trying to catch up to me.

The two inches of snow that fell last night turned the town into a winter wonderland. Snowflakes cling to the trees and rooftops creating a picturesque view of Evergreen Falls. Our small town looks like it could sit underneath a Christmas tree.

I march up the steps of Evergreen Savings and Loan like a soldier reporting for duty. Ever since Mr. Hooper, the owner of Evergreen Savings and Loan for as long as I can remember, sold out to some Wall Street hot shot, all the businesses in town are in danger. Mom and Dad built up our Christmas tree farm from nothing and there's no way in hell I'm going to lose it.

The sound of crumpling paper fills the air, courtesy of my death grip on the heartless one-page letter both Belle and I had received. Increasing interest rates, adding on bogus fees, and doing it two weeks before Christmas? Who is this guy, The Grinch?

Belle takes a second to catch her breath. "You're not on the all-county track team anymore." She hunches over and takes a few more deep breaths.

"Sorry, I speed walk when I'm focused." The fires of hell burning through me might have something to do with it, too. If we were still in high school and I was this hyped up I'd probably win the state championship for Evergreen Falls High.

Belle pulls the door handle of the old building. "Of course it's locked. With all these rules you'd think the new guy would be on time." Belle turns around and rests the back of her head on the door. She lets out a sigh. "I can't believe I'm losing my bakery."

I shake her arm. "Stop it right now. You are not losing the bakery and I'm not losing the tree farm. We're going to talk to this Gabriel guy and explain to him what his new rules will do to this town. I'm sure we can negotiate. That's what these Wall Street guys do, right?"

She shrugs her shoulder.

"Come on, Belle. You're acting like we've already lost. We've got to pull it together." I step to the side and wipe the fog off the window. Okay, so I'll pretend the red cheeks are from the cold rather than the hellfire rising inside. I tuck a few strands of my long brown hair behind an ear and plaster on a smile.

Belle gives her blonde ponytail a tug and smooths out the make-up under her eyes. She clearly hasn't gotten much sleep the last few days. None of us have. Who could blame her? She built Sugar Plum Bakery practically all by herself fresh out of culinary school. Everyone thought she'd head off to a big city and become an executive chef in a five star restaurant, but she came back right after graduation. Mr. Hooper loaned her the money to get started six months ago and her dream is finally a reality... for now.

I nibble my lip. "We're ready to take on the world." I try to hide the shakiness in my voice. Truth be told, if this guy doesn't want to play ball we've got serious problems. Mr. Hooper let us slide if we couldn't make our payments on time. His rates were lower than any I've ever seen. He wanted to help everyone in town survive, and live great lives. He is one of us. My family's Christmas tree farm would've gone under last year when Dad passed if Mr. Hooper hadn't helped us get back on our feet.

"Where is this guy? Is everything he does virtual or something?" Belle gazes along Main Street. Not a car on the road.

Once Mr. Hooper sold the savings and loan, Joanie, his secretary was fired two days later in an effort to save costs and modernize the business. Now this new guy wants everything done online or through zoom. A face to face meeting is the only way to hash things like this out here. I hate to break it to him, but I'll stand here until the end of time, if necessary.

"Don't worry, we'll work on our strategy while we wait." I pull out my candy apple red lip gloss from my pocket and slather it on.

"Really?" Belle lets out a chuckle.

I shrug. "Can't hurt." I smack my lips together. "Okay, should we go in together or attack separately?"

"Together." Belle flashes a smile. "Nat, we were called the Dynamic Duo for a reason."

I roll my eyes. "That was a volleyball tournament five years ago." We did beat ten other teams from all over the state. Maybe she has a point. It's like she can read my mind half the time anyway.

She nudges my arm. "Now who's the Debbie Downer? This guy has no chance against us, remember?"

I nod. "Definitely," I stand up tall, my shoulders back and my head up. "We're going to walk in there and demand Gabriel talk to us about these new regulations."

"Right." Belle stands tall next to me. She's two inches taller but I wore my platform boots so we're just about even. She gives the glass a quick rub with the arm of her jacket. "Look at us, no way he can resist."

I nod and take a deep breath, gazing at our reflection. This waiting game is killing me. I wish he'd get here already. I look down at the piece of paper that could ruin me. The hours printed at the bottom are the same as they've always been; 9am to 5pm. I glance down at my watch, It's 9:20 am. Either this guy doesn't care about his new business, or more than we thought has changed. I fold my arms across my chest and rotate from side to side, trying to shake off the cold. Belle covers her nose and mouth with her hands, blowing warm air. Freezing us out is a strategy I didn't anticipate.

Screeching tires rip through the air. We both jump at the same time. I look over onto Main Street and watch a shiny black Mustang fishtail across the snow-covered road. The rev of the engine blasts through the town like an atomic bomb.

Exhaust fumes flow toward me. I cover my face with my hand, coughing into my glove.

Belle waves her hand in front of her face. "Who the hell drives a muscle car in Evergreen Falls in the winter?"

I drop my hand. "An outsider."

The Mustang crawls its way to the parking lot of Evergreen Savings & Loan, and slides into a parking spot. Is this guy for real? I mean, you'd think you would research everything about the town before purchasing a property. He must be the worst businessman in the world. Clearly he knows nothing about how to prosper here, from his ideas he put in the letter.

Belle and I focus on the black car, following its every move. The engine shuts down. We stare, waiting for Satan to emerge.

I let out the breath I didn't realize I was holding. The car door opens and my heart pounds in my chest. I stare, frozen. Black shoes that look like they were bought ten minutes ago step out into the snow. He stands tall, at least six feet, and brushes off the few snowflakes that fall onto his long leather coat. Jeez, is he a business man or a Calvin Klein model? Perfectly chiseled face, dark hair just long enough to run your fingers through it, and a toned body not even a million layers of clothes can hide. Heat flutters through me and this time it has nothing to do with impending rage. He closes the car door and takes a step toward us, glancing at the building before focusing on us.

He waves. I wave back, a small smile forming the second we lock eyes. If his picture was on a billboard, Evergreen Falls would have the highest fender bender rate in the country.

"Are we killing him with kindness?" Belle huffs.

What the hell am I doing? Am I seriously letting my panties get in a bunch over the guy trying to destroy me? I've got to get it together. "No, sorry. I think the cold is freezing my brain."

"We're here to save our businesses... remember?" Belle paces in front of the door. "Don't let his hotness factor get to you."

I roll my eyes. "Please, give me more credit than that." Caught red handed. *Come on, Nat you're not that type of girl.* I guess it's been way too long since I've been on a date if the guy trying to ruin me is getting me all flustered. My cheeks are no doubt scarlet. At least I can blame it on the intense rage this letter is causing.

He walks up the steps and meets us at the door. "Ah, my first customers." He fumbles with his keys. "Hello Ladies. Sorry for being late. I hope you weren't waiting long." He flashes a smile that could bring the devil to his knees.

Belle shakes her head no.

Ah ha. I'm not the only one who's speechless. We'd better both get it together or this meeting is doomed.

He slides the key in the lock and opens the heavy door. He stands back and holds the door for us. The sneakiest of criminals can be a handsome gentleman. Look at Ted Bundy. Of course this Gabriel probably isn't even close to as smart.

"Thank you," I say as I glide inside.

Belle follows.

He shuts the door, leaving the cold behind us. "I guess you can take the guy out of L.A. but can't take L.A. out of the guy." He heads to the thermostat and cranks it up. "I'm Gabriel Carter. Let's head to my office and we can defrost."

Belle and I glance at each other and follow him to the door at the end of the hall. Ah, a California import. No wonder he has no clue about Evergreen Falls or the climate.

He slides off his coat and drapes it over an arm revealing a perfectly tailored suit. The kind that could be compared to lingerie on a woman. I fidget with my fingers. The only way this meeting is going to be useful is if I could find a way to go temporarily blind for the next twenty minutes.

He opens the door and hangs his coat on the coat rack to the right and leans against his desk, knocking over a picture onto the floor.

I bend over and grab it. Three guys stand shirtless holding surf boards, Gabriel in the center. Okay, I was wrong. Shirtless is a million times better than the suit. I follow the curves of his body getting lost in the photo.

Belle clears her throat.

I hand the photo to him, my hand trembling as he takes it.

"What can I help you with today? Surf lessons are my special-ty." He winks and leans on Mr. Hooper's cherry desk. The outlines of his muscles are clinging to the fine fabric, and just revealing enough to make any woman burst into flames.

I close my eyes for a second, trying to rip the image from my brain so it will function again. *Come on, Nat. Dig deep inside and bring out the raging grizzly bear about to protect her young.* I look up at him, gazing into his soft brown eyes. "I'm Natalie Watkins and I own Watkins' Tree Farm." Jesus, I sound like I just walked into AA.

He nods. "It's in the top three on my list of places to visit. I heard your tree farm has it all." He flashes a smile.

I take a deep breath. "Yes, we love it and it's one of the premier places to visit around Christmas time in Evergreen Falls." I nibble my lip.

Belle shakes her head and throws the crinkled letter on the desk next to him. "We're here to talk about this letter. You're going to ruin us all."

His eyes widen. He takes the letter and irons it out on his desk with his hands. "It's just a standard rate and policy letter. No big deal."

Yep, that's just what those Wall Street types think, they can throw their "standard" documents at us as if we can just adjust to the way the big city runs things. So I was wrong about the New York City but L.A. is pretty much the same deal. Did he buy the Savings & Loan to run it into the ground and bring in big box store retailers? Probably. L.A. is all about fancy and expensive stores.

I ball my hands into fists. "Mr. Hooper helped us run and keep our businesses. Evergreen Falls is a small town, not a city. We can't afford these rate hikes and fees. What, do you think you pulled into Rodeo Drive?"

He holds up his hands. "Whoa. These are still great rates and the fees are all standard. It's under the national average. I didn't buy this business to lose money." He runs a hand through his hair. "And I know there's not a Hollywood sign outside. I want to try something different."

I throw my hands in the air. "Like what, create a ghost town? Don't you get it? You're going to make all of us lose our businesses with your standard fees." I make the quote sign with my fingers and pace the length of his desk. "You come in here with your flashy car, that doesn't do so well in the snow by the way, and flaunt your designer clothes like we're all going to fall all over you. Well, you don't know this town at all. The car didn't help you out too much did it? And those good looks don't work either."

Dear god did I just say that out loud? Heat spreads across my cheeks like wildfire. Only a DeLorean and Flux capacitor can help me now.

Belle lowers her eyebrows and gives me that you've-got-to-be-kidding-me look. "Anyway, I think you should rethink your business strategy. I own Sugar Plum Bakery. Mr. Hooper helped me get my business started and I'm finally turning a decent profit, but I can't afford this." She points to the letter. "He let me slide on six months of payments which I'm making up now. But these rates would have me paying triple what I pay now just to catch up."

"Exactly." Finally my brain regained its function. "It's Christmas time here. The whole town comes together. We have so many events and functions these next two weeks. It's time for us to prosper, not fold."

He stands up and blows air out of his cheeks. "Okay, I get it. This letter was a shock to you and Mr. Hooper did things differently."

Knocking emanates through the air along with muffled voices.

He scrunches his eyebrows and heads out of his office to the front door. "What is going on?" He mutters under his breath.

Belle and I follow.

"It's about time the blood made its way back to your brain." Belle nudges me.

"Shut up." Okay, so I started off a bit shaky but I'm back to my bad ass self.

Gabriel steps into the foyer greeted by an angry mob. Each of them holding the letter in their hand. The only thing they're missing is fire lit torches.

"Please, give me a chance to explain." Gabriel holds up his hands as if he's about to be taken down by the local police force. Ironically, they're the only ones in town who aren't here.

Miss Jenners steps forward. "I own the Evergreen Bed and Breakfast and with the increasing food and heating costs, I can't afford another hiked up bill. If I have to pay these kinds of rates I might as well use one of those national mortgage companies. No reason to keep my business in town."

"I understand." Gabriel yells, trying to cut through the crowd. "This is all standard and I'm still cheaper than those companies."

"I might go with one of those companies and pay a little more than stay with you. You're going to put a lot of us out of business. It's not right. You should go down too," Jake from The Blue Cat Restaurant yells.

An array of cheers fill the air.

"You just waltz in here and think you're going to starve us all. Well we are not going to let you do it." Nancy from Evergreen Dry Cleaners steps to the front of the crowd. "We're not corporate chains here. We all built our businesses from the ground up. Hard work and dedication and we all help each other. You're in small town U.S.A, not some metropolis."

"I understand. We can all discuss this together. Maybe we can set up a zoom meeting." Gabriel takes a step back.

Groans and even a few curse words fill the air. "What is wrong with you, bud? We don't do zoom meetings here. We have face to face council meetings. Hell, some of us aren't even on Facebook."

He hangs his head and nods. "Okay, I get it. Things are done differently here. I'm here because I wanted a change and I'm ready to do just that." He lifts his head and stares at the angry crowd. "Let's set up a meeting where we can all discuss our concerns, but I can assure you, this is the best place to keep your loans."

Antonio, the owner of Vesuvius, our only upscale restaurant in town, steps forward. "The problem is that you are making changes without knowing your customers. That never works. Maybe you should get to know the people and the town before coming up with any new rules. Then we can decide what we're going to do."

Gabriel points at Antonio. "You're right." He turns toward me and we lock eyes for a split second. He walks over to me. "Natalie from Watkins Tree Farm is going to show me around town and explain to me how everything works. Then we'll talk and work all of this out."

Wait, what?

CHAPTER 2

TRADITIONS

I'M JUST GOING TO WALK IN THERE IN TELL HIM HE'S ON HIS OWN. Why on Earth did he think he could drag me into his battle with the town? I mean, hello, I'm on their side, not his. I stand up tall and take a deep cleansing breath. Okay, here I go.

I pull open the door of the Blue Cat Restaurant with so much force the bell rings twice. Nothing like making my entrance known. Jake spots me from behind the counter. I flash a smile and he points to the right.

Gabriel sits in the last booth on the far side of the restaurant. Well, at least we're hidden. Probably the best idea since pretty much everyone in town is out for his blood. I follow the black and white tiles, glancing at the blue cat adorning the wall. Jake's daughter painted it when he opened a few years ago. Now she's in art school in Chicago. Who knows, maybe she'll become famous and put Evergreen Falls on the map.

I take off my coat and slide into the booth.

Gabriel jumps, sloshing his coffee to the rim of the cup. "Sorry, I didn't see you." He stands up. "Thanks for coming."

Ah, a gentleman. It's probably just instinct from being in the corporate world. Guys like him are experts at hiding their true self, but once it shows up, all hell breaks loose.

"Has your brain function returned? You went pretty crazy last time I saw you." I grab a menu.

He sits down. "Listen, I'm sorry. I shouldn't have just volunteered you but my life was at stake. It was a dire situation. I needed a hero." He tilts his head and stares at me with puppy dog eyes.

My heart instantly races the second we lock eyes. Does he have this effect on every girl or am I somehow susceptible to his charms. "Really? Does that line ever work?"

"Every time." He flashes a smile. "In all seriousness, once I said you'd work with me everyone calmed down. It's like Valium was pumped into the air."

I roll my eyes. "Yeah, because everyone trusts me and I'm sure as hell not going to betray that to help you. Besides, what good is any of this for me? I'm part of the angry mob, remember?"

He runs a hand through his hair. Tingles sweep through me. Dammit. How can I want to kill him and tackle him to the ground and have my way with him all at the same time? I'm starting to think Belle was right when she said he was a demon summoned here.

He holds up a finger. "Great point." He pulls out a legal pad and pen. "I crunched the numbers for your tree farm. Mr. Hooper helped you out by loaning you extra money, not charging any late fees, and keeping the interest rates at ridiculously low levels. No wonder he sold, he'd probably run himself out of business in a few months."

I ball my hands into fists. "Mr. Hooper moved to Florida to take care of his sick mother. He wasn't out to drain the town so he could drive fancy sports cars and wear thousand dollar suits. He would've done just fine if he didn't have to leave." I throw my hands in the air. "That's your problem. Not everything can be calculated and crunching numbers isn't reality."

Jake comes over and sets a cup of coffee in front of me. "Thought you could use this, Nat. Everything alright?"

I nod. "Thanks Jake."

He stares at Gabriel and then back at me. "Let me know if you need anything."

I flash a smile and Jake walks away.

"Lesson number one. We stick together here. You mess with one of us, you mess with all of us." I pour a creamer into my coffee and take a sip.

"Yep, he looks like he wants to rip my head off. Noted." He takes his pen and points to an array of equations. "Let's say I left the rate the same. If you could pay an extra ten percent a month on our loan you'd cut off five years."

"Great, if I could pay extra anything I wouldn't need you or your savings and loan." Does he think I have hidden streams of money?

"Just hear me out. What if we had a few events at your tree farm? From my research, they pull in a ton of profit this time of year and you could add it to your loan in a lump sum each year to work against the principal. Plus, you get more publicity and can expand your goods and services."

Okay, all of that sounds great but things working on paper and things working in real life are very different. Plus, we barely have the manpower to run the farm now. How the hell am I going to man all these events? Hiring more people and paying them would diminish any of the potential profits. I don't have a business degree but it just doesn't add up.

"So what exactly are you proposing?" I slide my coffee cup over and pull the legal notebook toward me. His fingers brush mine, sending an array of tingles through my body like a lightning strike.

"You show me around, walk me through the town's events, and help me gain everyone's trust so we can talk about moving forward and I will set up the events I'm talking about at your farm and show you how you can take the farm to the next level. It's a win-win for both of us." He sips his coffee.

"Gabriel."

He holds up his hand. "Please, call me Gabe."

I let out a breath. "Okay, Gabe. I can't risk any money on whatever events you're thinking of having. We are swamped handling the normal daily chores to stay up and running. Plus we already have the Gingerbread Competition at the farm. It might be way too much."

"I'll assume all of the risk and it won't cost you a dime. As for manpower, you got me. It's going to help both of us. I promise." He holds out his hand to shake mine. "Please give me a chance."

What, does he think he can do the job of an army? It's clear Mr. Surfer Boy has no clue how much work is involved. Ugh, I could really use help making the farm more prosperous. He seems like he knows what he's talking about unless he's the king of all bullshitters. I nibble my lip. What the hell.

I shake his hand. "Okay, I'll do it to help Evergreen Falls." My stomach falls to the ground. Did I just make a deal with the devil?

～

"JUMP IN THE CAR, WE'RE HEADING TO THE EVERGREEN Psychiatric hospital." Belle grabs a bottle of water from the fridge and sits on one of the stools of the island.

"Come on, I have to do something or we're never going to get out of this mess. You want to keep your bakery, right?" I take off my hat and toss it onto the counter. "Shouldn't you be thanking me?"

She shrugs. "I guess. It just seems so wrong to buddy up with him."

"Whatever works. Don't you remember that saying 'Keep your friends close and your enemies closer'? This kind of stuff is what it applies to."

"You're a better woman than I. If it was up to me I'd put Ex-Lax in his hot chocolate."

"If it goes sour that's not a bad idea."

We both burst out laughing.

Clyde, our number one farmhand and Belle's boyfriend, walks in. "Trees are ready for sale. Great crop this year. Take a look and see what you think." He gives Belle a quick peck on the cheek. "I saved you the perfect one for the bakery."

Belle's smile could light up the whole farmhouse. It's been dismal here since Dad passed. Even this time of year, the lights don't seem to shine as bright as they used to. And now Mom is the star of the show, with me as the supporting actress. Maybe these events Gabe is planning will add some cheer. We could all use some of it.

"Clyde, why don't you drop Belle's tree off at the bakery and head to the Evergreen Hardware. Jenna has an order ready for us. Got to spruce things up for the big Gingerbread Competition. I think someone might have her eye on the prize." I wink at Belle.

"I might have a few things up my sleeve." She jumps off the stool and grabs her bottle of water. "Catch ya later. You going on a date with Satan today?"

I shake my head. "No, not until the Gingerbread Competition." I huff. "And it's not a date. It is all business."

"Sure it is." She raises an eyebrow and heads out the door with Clyde.

"Did I hear right? You have a date?" My mom walks down the steps in her Christmas sweater and black pants. She always wears a festive outfit the day we get the trees ready for sale. A small smile graces her face.

"No, not a date. Just a business meeting with the guy who took over after Mr. Hooper." I head over to counter and grab a stack of price tags for the trees.

"Ah, yes. He's the talk of the town." She grabs a few sharpies from the drawer and heads to the kitchen table. "What are you planning?"

Great question. I slide into the kitchen chair and take one of the sharpies. "I'm not sure yet. I told him I'd show him around town so he can meet everyone and in exchange he'll help me expand business here by hosting some events. Don't worry, I'll run everything by you first."

She puts her hand on mine. "I trust you." She slides her hand away and puts on her glasses. "Dolores from the market told me he's sex in a suit."

"Mom!"

She shrugs. "I'm just telling you what people are saying."

I catch a glimpse of my face from the mirror in the hutch across from us. Pure scarlet. "He's very handsome, not that it matters."

"It certainly doesn't hurt." She holds in a smile.

"It's not a date, just business." Alright so he's a cross between Chris Hemsworth and Keanu Reeves. And I don't mind looking at him, but we are working together, not hooking up.

"Let's forget about him and get our trees ready. I've got $29.99 tags and $39.99 tags. Clyde bragged about the crop this year. I guess our new fertilizer did the trick." I grab the finished tags and hop out of the chair.

"Best trees I've seen in years." Mom finishes her last tag and gathers them up to put on the trees.

We grab our coats and head outside.

"Okay, Clyde has the larger ones on the left and the shorter ones on the right. Let's get tagging." I stick the first few tags on the trees.

The smell of fresh cut pine fills the air. I take a deep breath. The soft branches graze my fingers as I work. I take a step back and look at the rows of trees, illuminated by the Christmas lights strung around the wooden corral. If Santa and his reindeer were here, you'd think you were in the North Pole.

Rustling comes from behind me. I turn and see one of the trees shaking back and forth. Did a squirrel already make a home in one of these beauties? Mom comes over to my row, she must've heard it too.

The tree moves to and fro like a great white shark has a hold of it. Mom gasps. I run over to the tree and grab it before it falls over. An array of pine needles swoop through my hair. Leather gloves grasp my hands. Before I have a chance to scream, warm eyes meet with mine.

Gabe moves his head to the side of the branches. "Spectacular."

I loosen my grip. "You almost gave me a heart attack." I let out a breath and take a step back.

"Stopping pretty girls' hearts is my specialty." He steps out from behind the tree and flashes a smile.

Mom puts out her hand. "I'm Carol, Natalie's mom. I'm guessing you're Gabriel."

He shakes her hand. "Call me Gabe." He moves his head from right to left. "Your tree farm is amazing. And this beauty," he gestures to the tree and then shifts his eyes toward me "is perfect."

Heat sweeps through me.

"I couldn't agree more." Mom puts an arm around me. "It's on the house."

Gabe shakes his head. "No way, I'm a paying customer. I think I picked a great one for my first real Christmas tree."

I scrunch my eyebrows. "Really?" Jeez, I shouldn't act so surprised. Maybe his religion doesn't celebrate Christmas. "I mean. Do you celebrate Hanukkah? We can use blue and silver decorations."

"No. We had a tabletop artificial tree. Nothing much. My family was more into New Year's."

Mom walks over to Gabe and puts a hand on his shoulder. "Come on in for some hot cocoa. It's the best in town," she smiles.

"I could never resist anything chocolate."

"Natalie, get Gabe's tree ready and we'll meet you inside." She pushes the tree in my direction and intertwines her arm with Gabe's. They walk toward the farmhouse. Mom turns her head back and raises her eyebrows giving me that Oh-my-god-he's-so-handsome look.

I stumble, catching myself before dropping the tree. Does his charm work on all women, or just the Watkins girls?

I'd better move. God knows what Mom's telling him. With my luck she'll be pulling out my baby pictures. I grab the tree and take it over to the loading area, where I throw on the tree net and tighten it up. Okay, there's no way I can tie it to his roof without the keys. I bet it'll be the only tree attached to the roof of a Mustang I see this whole holiday season. I almost want to snap a photo.

The image of me as a baby in the bathtub flashes through my mind, I'd better get in the house… now. I trot over to the house and storm inside like I'm about to invade.

Mom sets down her mug and lowers her eyebrows. "Every-thing okay?"

I nod and rip off my coat, dropping a few of the tags out of my pocket. "Could really use some of that cocoa."

"Uh… okay." Mom gets up from the table and pours me a cup.

I slide in the chair opposite Gabe.

He takes a sip of cocoa. "Best thing I've tasted since I got here."

Mom hands me the mug and joins us at the table. "Secret recipe, passed down three generations."

Okay, maybe he should finish his cocoa and go on his way. It's kinda strange that someone who never had a live Christmas tree before heads over to the farm to get one. Is he trying to fit in, or does he have ulterior motives? He's got to be up to something.

I put my detective skills to work. "What brings you here tonight, anyway? Did you want first pick of a tree?"

"If I knew about this cocoa, I'd have been here sooner." He takes another sip and wipes a bit of froth off his top lip. "I'm checking out the town and heard buzz about this amazing tree farm up the road so I figured I'd check it out."

"Buzz? From who?" I gulp my cocoa.

"Natalie," Mom gives me the side eye. "Well, we're glad you stopped by." She sips her cocoa. "So, Gabe. You're from California?"

"Yes ma'am. Los Angeles."

"Ah, the land of sunshine and sand. Here you are, in the snow and the cold. What brings you to Evergreen Falls? It's so different to L.A."

He finishes the last drop of cocoa. Jeez, it's like he wants to lick the mug. "Exactly. I wanted something completely new. A break from the crowds and corporate world. I was searching for small town financial institutions for sale and came across this savings and loan. When I researched Evergreen Falls I was hooked. It's like a land in a storybook."

The way he's going it's going to be the land in a book authored by Stephen King.

"Best town in the world." Gabe better keep it that way.

Mom nods.

"I took a chance and packed up. I didn't realize my standard letter would make me public enemy number one. I guess I have a lot to learn about small town life." He shifts his eyes toward me. "I'm lucky I met Natalie."

Tingles invade my body. No doubt my cheeks are redder than Santa's. "Mom, I agreed to show Gabe around town and try to explain to everyone he's not Satan and he's going to organize a few events here at the farm to increase our business."

"Really, they're calling me Satan?"

Just Belle and I but he doesn't need to know that. "It's not important."

Mom stands up and gathers our cups. "I've got a great idea."

She puts the cups in the sink. "Gabe, were you planning on coming to the Gingerbread Competition? It's one of our biggest Christmas events."

"Yes. Natalie told me a little about it. I was planning on stopping by all of the booths." Gabe stands up and pulls his keys out of his pocket.

Okay, he's ready to leave. I think we've had enough small talk for today. With my luck, Mom will be inviting him to dinner if I don't get him out of here.

I rush over and grab my coat. "I've got your tree all ready. Just need to tie it to the roof." The sooner he leaves the better, before she starts telling us all of her ideas.

"Natalie judges the contests every year. How about this year we have two judges? Gabe, would you do us the honor?"

All the air leaves my body. Great, I'm Satan's sidekick. Thanks Mom.

CHAPTER 3

GINGERBREAD COMPETITION

"I can't believe you found a surfing Santa sweater." I try not to smile as I peruse the blue sweater with Santa in board shorts and his Santa hat catching a wave.

Gabe pulls down the bottom hem of his sweater and looks down. "Please, it's gnarly."

The tradition is everyone here at the farm wears a Christmas sweater on Gingerbread Competition day. Every year I pull out a favorite one that Dad got me back when he went on an Alaskan cruise with mom. It's Merry Christmoose, a moose with a Santa hat. I guess it's kinda of cool that Gabe is joining in the town's traditions. He doesn't have to do all of this but he cares enough to try and become one of us. I guess that's going above and beyond to make his business thrive.

I grab a Santa hat from the kitchen counter and hand one to Gabe. "Okay, here's the deal. Everyone has a booth set up and it's our job to judge their gingerbread houses based on three factors. First, the taste of their sample desserts; second, creativity; and third, technical skill."

"Doesn't Belle have this in the bag since she owns a bakery?"

He takes the Santa hat and pulls it on, tossing the pom-pom ball to the right.

My heart rate instantly increases. Even with the surfing Santa sweater, he looks like he could melt all the snow outside with his hotness factor. Sexiest Santa I've ever seen.

"Ready guys?" Mom steps into the kitchen, pulling me out of the thoughts that were destined to put me on the naughty list.

"Yep." I put on my hat and grab two notepads and pens, handing one to Gabe. "You'd think the baker has the upper hand but you'd be surprised."

Mom walks outside and turns on the Christmas music. *Jingle Bell Rock* flows through the air.

I head to the door but Gabe stands still. I turn back to see what's causing the hold up. I focus on his perfectly tailored jeans that hug all the curves of his body and continue up to the surfing Santa shirt, finally stopping at the flawless jawline that seems to be clenched.

"You coming?" I tilt my head and lower my eyebrows.

"Are you sure this is a good idea? I mean, won't the ones who don't win hate me even more? I'm trying to win them over, not give them an excuse to chase me down with torches."

I walk over to him and put a hand on his shoulder. "Everyone knows this is all in fun. It looks good that you're here and taking an interest. That's what everyone cares about, not who is chosen as the winner." I take his hand and pull him toward the door. Shockwaves surge through my body the second our skin touches. I take my hand away and grab the two pairs of gloves from the table, handing one to Gabe. "Except Belle, she might be out for blood." I nudge him with my arm.

All the concern in his face disappears into a smile. "Why do I feel like I'm going to be dodging flying candy canes?"

"I have seen her throw a fruitcake."

He slides the pen behind an ear and puts on his gloves, gripping the notepad. "Let's get this party started."

I open the door and we head outside. It's warmer than normal, about fifty degrees. I take in a deep breath and let the crisp air invigorate my senses. Colored lights illuminate every stand and the smell of baked goods fills the air.

Gabe's eyes light up like a kid on Christmas morning. "This is amazing". He steps out into the aisle filled with booths on both sides. "Merry Christmas everyone," he waves.

"Merry Christmas," said by a multitude of voices fills the air.

Wait, didn't he say his family wasn't into Christmas? Could've fooled me, he's acting like Buddy the Elf took over his body.

"We'll go to each booth together. Judging is based on a one to ten scale with ten being the best. I have the pages set up by booth number and category. Got it?" I flip open the pad to page one.

"Aye, Aye Captain." He gives me a military salute.

We walk over to the first booth, Sugar Plum Bakery. Belle gives Gabe the once over, looking him up and down. "Nice shirt, Surfer Boy."

"Santa's always down to hang ten." He makes the hang ten gesture with his hand.

Belle steps to the side to unveil her gingerbread creation.

Gabe's mouth falls open. A gingerbread castle stands on the table in front of us. It's truly a work of art. A moat of piping gel runs around it and under the drawbridge. Gumdrops make stained glass windows throughout the towers and a dragon 3-D cookie, decorated with such fine detail you'd almost think it's real, stands before a princess cookie. "I've never seen anything like this… it's unreal."

"Really cool, Belle. Very creative, but it's not screaming Christmas." I jot down a few notes in my pad.

"What? Look at the Christmas lights on the tower." Belle points to the multicolored dots strung along the gingerbread castle.

"Ah, almost missed them." I jot down a few more notes. I can see the steam rising from Belle. Maybe this will be Gabe's time to shine.

"You're crazy. It's insane and perfect. I mean, it has it all. The dragon and the princess are celebrating together in the true spirit of Christmas. How did you miss it?" Gabe stares at Belle's creation like an art enthusiast stares at a painting.

The smile Belle was fighting to hold in breaks free. "See? Surfer Boy gets it."

"Well, it's a step up from Satan," Gabe whispers to me.

I roll my eyes. "Beautiful work, Belle." I point to the fireplace shaped cookies on the tray near the side of her table. "Is that the tasting element?"

She nods her head and brings over the tray. "Decorated ginger-bread fireplaces with a hint of spice from our fire breathing dragon."

Gabe grabs one and sticks the whole thing in his mouth. "Wow. If everything you make is this good I'd better buy stock in the bakery. It's sweet and savory all at the same time. I could eat the whole tray." He sticks his hand out to grab another cookie.

I stop him mid-reach. "We have a lot more samples to taste." I gesture toward the row of booths waiting to be judged. "You don't want to fill up."

He rubs his chin. "Is that a challenge?"

I shake my head and smile. "Come on, on to the next contestant."

Gabe heads to the next booth. I start walking but Belle grabs my arm before I make it out of her reach. "What did you do to Surfer Boy? He's acting... human."

I shrug. "Maybe the three ghosts visited him."

Belle looks over at Gabe. He turns back and nods his head to the side, gesturing me to join him. I smile and put up my pointer finger in a one-minute fashion.

"Ah ha. Or maybe Cupid hit him with an arrow." Belle raises her eyebrows.

"Not even close. I already told you, this is all business. Plus, it seems like it's working. He's a big fan of Sugar Plum Bakery, right? You can thank me later." I rush off before she can say anything else.

What is she thinking? Just because Gabe is handsome, and funny, and charming doesn't mean I'm going to fall all over him. Did she forget he walked in here trying to ruin us? Sure, he's on his way to make things right but that doesn't erase everything else.

I shake off her comments and move on to the next booth. It's Antonio from Vesuvius.

"Natalie, you've got to see this." Gabe points to Antonio's gingerbread house. It's a replica of the Roman Colosseum, complete with a lion and gladiator cookie inside. Christmas lights made from icing hang on the top of the structure and Christmas stocking decorations are on the entrances inside. A 3-D Christmas tree made from cookies stands tall in the middle of the arena rising up to the top.

Whoa, this is the most elaborate gingerbread house I've ever seen. I guess Antonio is in it to win it. I bend down and peek my head around the array of perfectly arched windows, each one with a candle decoration in the middle.

"I could stare at this all day." Gabe moves from side to side, staring at the gingerbread creation.

"Thank you both so much. I wanted to bring Christmas in Italy to Christmas in Evergreen Falls and add in a little history too." Antonio pulls out a tray of reindeer shaped cookies. "Try my Mostaccioli cookies."

Gabe has the cookie in his mouth before I can even grab mine. His eyes widen. "Antonio, this is the best thing I've ever tasted. I've never been to Italy but if the food there is half as good as this I need to get on a plane right now."

Antonio raises his hands. "Thank you so much. It's a family

recipe passed down for generations. My grandmother used to make these for us every year on Christmas Eve."

I take a bite and close my eyes. The flavors of ginger, hazelnut, and honey invade my senses. Gabe is right, it's the best cookie I've ever tasted. Maybe he should nix the business degree and become a food taster.

"Absolutely delicious, Antonio and a beautiful display. Thank you." I jot a few notes in my pad.

Gabe grabs another cookie. "You should seriously sell these. They're unique and amazing."

"Hmm." Antonio places a finger to his lip. "Who knows, maybe you'll see it on the menu of Vesuvius."

I grab Gabe's arm and pull him to the next booth before he eats the whole tray of cookies. "I didn't think someone with a body like yours would have a major sweet tooth." Dear God, did I just say that out loud?

"Ms. Watkins, are you scoping out my hot bod?" he winks.

Heat flushes through my cheeks like a volcanic explosion. "No... I mean... you're fit. You know, healthy." I fidget with my fingers. "I saw your surfing picture. You know, the one on your desk. It didn't look like any one of you had eaten a carb in years." Oh God, Natalie. Shut up, you're babbling.

"Ah ha. You were checking me out." He nudges my arm.

I sigh. "Just making an observation."

"Just so you know, I do eat carbs." He flashes a smile on our way to the next booth.

"I've only seen you drink coffee and Mom's hot chocolate, but no one can resist that." When we met at the Blue Cat Restaurant our meeting was over before our cup of coffee.

We step up to the next booth. "Maybe we should change that."

Chills sweep through my body. Did he just ask me out? Nah, I'm probably misinterpreting. He probably wants to eat something non-gingerbread.

"Hey Jake. I love this, a replica of the Blue Cat Restaurant." I peek into the window. Decorations made from icing mimic the inside of the restaurant, right down to the blue cat mural on the wall. Little booths made out of gingerbread fill the inside. Hey, there's the booth Gabe and I sat at for our meeting.

Am I seriously getting nostalgic about going to the Blue Cat with Gabe? I've got to be losing my mind. Maybe there's more in these gingerbread samples than meets the eye.

Gabe bends down, scanning the intricate confection. "Is the Christmas tree decorated with little blue cat ornaments?"

"Yes, sir," says Jake.

I scan the gingerbread diner and spot the Christmas tree inside made out of cookies and decorated with royal icing blue cats. It's magnificent. How did I miss that? Gabe stands up and runs a hand through his hair. Ah, maybe that has something to do with it. Why did I make this deal with him again? Oh yeah, to save the town. Who's going to save me?

Jake hands us each a blue cat cookie. "All American hot cocoa gingerbread cookie."

I take a bite and accidentally moan out loud. The chocolate with the spices of the gingerbread is amazing. Jake cooked back in his military days for his platoon. One bite of these and the line would to enlist would be miles long.

Gabe eats the cookie in two bites. He holds his hands in the air. "Sorry, Nat. This is all you. I can't choose a winner. They're all the best thing I've ever tasted." He flashes that sexy half-smile that should be outlawed.

I shake my head. "Fine, you're off the hook." Since when did he start calling me Nat?

"Hot chocolate for the judges?" Mom sneaks up behind us with a tray of hot chocolate.

Gabe grabs one like he's just emerged from a desert and is dying of thirst. "I think this is one of the best days of my life." He takes a sip.

"Natalie has that effect on people." Mom smiles.

"She definitely does," Gabe says in between sips.

Heat sweeps across my face like she just blasted me with a blow torch. Maybe I would've been in better shape if she did. I stare at her with hellfire eyes. "Cute, Mom."

She scurries away with her hot chocolate tray. What is her deal anyway? Shouldn't she be carrying the torches with the rest of the town trying to hang Gabe? Selling my soul to Satan isn't the answer. I look over at Gabe, a foam mustache covering his top lip. A smile forms across my face. Okay, so maybe he's not Satan. He's more like a high-level demon.

Gabe wipes his mouth. "Where do we go from here?"

Isn't that the million-dollar question? Right, the Gingerbread Competition. I flip open my notebook. "We compare notes and add up the points in each category to choose a winner."

He presses his lips together. "I've got everything right here." He puts a finger on his temple.

"So, you didn't take any notes and pretty much just walked around eating cookies."

He nods, "Yeah, and it was awesome."

A chuckle escapes. "What am I going to do with you?"

"I can't wait to find out." He slugs down the rest of his hot chocolate.

Butterflies form in my stomach. I take a breath. He's probably just wondering about the next town event. Yeah, that's probably it. "Let's head to the kitchen and see what's in my notebook. And in your head even though I'm scared to find that one out." I nudge his arm.

He opens his mouth to say something but then holds up his hand and smiles. "I'm not touching that one."

We head into the kitchen. I pull off my coat and take a seat on the stool near the island. Gabe unzips his jacket and slowly pulls it off. My eyes follow the curves of his muscles, dancing underneath the green fabric of his thermal shirt.

"Earth to Natalie." He slides his jacket on the back of the stool.

I jerk, pulling myself back into reality. "Just going through the entries for the competition, you know, in my head." My cheeks must be crimson.

He raises his eyebrows. "See, I'm bringing something to the judging."

Yep, more than I bargained for. I slide my notepad between us. "Here's the scores I came up with. See what you think."

He leans in to get a closer look. His soft breath flows across my cheek, blowing a few strands of hair to and fro. The scent of hot chocolate and his musky cologne sends tingles through my body. My heart beats on overdrive.

He slowly picks his head up, locking eyes with mine.

I close my eyes for a second and my brain kicks back in. What is happening? I open my eyes and lean away, knocking myself off the stool. I catch myself right before I plummet to the floor.

"Are you okay?" Gabe grabs my arm, pulling me back onto the stool.

"Yep, I guess I'd better fix the leg on that stool." I take a few breaths. "So, based on the scores, it looks like Antonio from Vesuvius is the winner." I wiggle in the seat and run a hand through my hair and try to pull myself together.

He nods. "Great choice."

I hop off the stool and grab my coat, throwing it on and zipping it up in one swoop. "Let's announce the results."

Gabe puts on his coat. I look at my notepad, trying to avoid eye contact with his body. I doubt I can make more of a fool of myself than I already have but no reason to challenge it. We head outside and meet my mom in the middle aisle.

"Thank you all so much for taking part in the Gingerbread Competition. It was a really hard decision this year. Everyone has gone above and beyond, and you all should be proud." I pull the gift card from my pocket.

Gabe chimes in, "Best cookies I've tasted in my life and I've

AMY L. GALE

been all over the world. Evergreen Falls is an amazing place. Thank you for letting me be a part of it all."

Everyone breaks out into clapping. Okay, he either really means it or he missed his calling and should go back to L.A. to become an actor.

"Antonio you are the winner. Please accept this Watkin's Tree Farm gift card and we will display your gingerbread house. Congratulations." I give Antonio a hug and hand him the gift card.

"Thank you so much." He kisses me on both cheeks.

Gabe holds out his hand to shake Antonio's but Antonio pulls him into a hug.

"I want to see both of you at my restaurant." Antonio stands in front of us, a big smile upon his face.

"I'd love to try Vesuvius. What do you say, Natalie? Do you want to go to dinner Saturday night?"

Wait, what did he just ask me?

"Sure you do. I'll save the best table for you two kids. See you Saturday, at seven." Antonio walks over to Mom who hands him the gingerbread house trophy she had made for the event.

What the hell just happened?

CHAPTER 4

DATE NIGHT?

Plastic hangers slide across the rod in my closet, clanking together like bumper cars. How do I keep getting myself in these situations? It's like aliens take over my brain whenever I'm around Gabe. Maybe I got it wrong and he's an extra-terrestrial, not the antichrist. I fiddle through my clothes trying to find something—anything—appropriate.

Dating is not my strong suit. A low growl escapes. Come on, Nat, this is a professional engagement and not a date. Either way, it's been a while. Last time I was at Vesuvius with a guy was when Les Johnson, whose family owns the sawmill, took me here for our break-up dinner. Two years of dating and he drops me for a girl he met online. A glass of wine thrown in his face sealed the deal. And to think he took me to the place we had our first date to dump me. Jerk.

Doesn't matter, Mom needed me more than ever at the farm, and I had all the time in the world to help her, since Les was out of the picture. In the hidden depths of my closet I stop at a black dress. Belle bought this for me when she was trying to play matchmaker and set me up on dates. I didn't oblige, but the store had a no return policy so the dress lived in the shadows. I pull it out and hold it up. The black silky fabric catches just a glimpse of light. It's classic with a hint of sexiness. Not exactly what I was looking for but it's either this or a flannel shirt with jeans. I lay the dress on my bed and cut off the sales tag. Gabe better not think this is a date.

I hop down the steps, putting on my black pumps in the process. A split-second later, knocking on the door resonates through the air.

Mom heads over to open it, but stops in front of me. "Natalie, you look beautiful. I can't remember the last time I saw you all dolled up for a date."

I head over to the coat closet to retrieve my only dress coat. "Not a date, just dinner."

"Ah ha." She smiles.

I roll my eyes.

Mom opens the door. "Nice to see you, Gabe."

He pulls a bouquet of red roses adorned with gold glitter from behind his back. "Likewise."

I stomp over to him. "It's just dinner, not a date. No need for flowers." I put my hand out to take them.

"Sorry, they're for Carol." He pulls the flowers out of my reach and hands them to my mom.

"Oh dear. It's been forever since someone brought me flowers." She gives him a kiss on the cheek. "Thank you."

I turn to mom. Her face is lit up like a Christmas tree. Well played, Gabe.

"They're beautiful, thank you." I flash a meek smile and grab my red wool dress coat from the coat rack and put it on.

"You kids have fun." Mom scurries to find a vase for her flowers.

"You look amazing. Am I allowed to tell you that Ms. Watkins?" Gabe flashes that sexy half smile that can instantly make your panties drop.

"I'm not sure, but thank you." I sling my purse over a shoulder and head out the door.

Gabe places his hand in the small of my back to guide me to the car. I should pull away and tell him this is a professional dinner, nothing more, but it kind of feels nice to get all dressed up and have a man actually act like a gentleman. Who knows? Maybe tonight can banish the bad memories from Vesuvius and I can head over more often to enjoy the amazing cuisine.

Gabe opens the door of his Mustang. "Your chariot awaits."

I slide in and close the door. Gabe steps to the other side and joins me. He fires up the engine. It roars like a lion.

"How many horses run in this chariot?"

"Four hundred and thirty-five," Gabe fiddles with the heat.

"Nice. If they were real horses it would be unstoppable in the snow." I turn on the radio.

"Don't hate the wheels. And please, go easy on my ears." He winks and pulls out.

"The wheels rock, just like my taste in music." I turn to the classic rock channel. *Rock and Roll all Night* by KISS flows through the airwaves.

"Nice, I saw them back in L.A. The show was amazing." He turns it up louder.

"I haven't had the pleasure but it's on my bucket list." I sway to the music.

"A rocker chick in Evergreen Falls. You know you're full of surprises."

"I'm just getting started."

His eyes widen.

Where the hell did that come from? Not the kind of talk that's going to make Gabe believe this is not a date. I've got to turn this conversation around. "I'm also not one of those girls who only order a salad and barely eat."

"Good." He looks over at me and then back at the road. "Just

33

so you know, guys who like to eat as much as I do, hate that. We need a partner in crime."

"Guess tonight's your lucky night." I cover my hand with my mouth and then quickly drop it. Jeez, are my brain cells on strike. I take a deep breath and silently pray he didn't take that out of context.

The lights lining the perimeter of Vesuvius shine like a beacon in the dark. Thank God we're here. Another minute in the car alone with Gabe and I'd be promising him a lap dance or something.

He turns the wheel and pulls into the parking lot. I gaze at the large, brick building adorned with red, white, and green Christmas lights. The red awning covering a cobblestone walkway reads *Vesuvius* in large white letters.

"Nice place. It reminds me of somewhere I used to go with my family back in L.A. every year for Mom's birthday." Gabe shuts down the engine.

"Fanciest restaurant in town." I open my door. The sooner I get out, the better.

"Wait a minute." Gabe hops out of the car and rushes over to the other side. He holds open the car door and puts out his hand to take mine. "I know, not a date, but I was raised to be a gentleman."

I take his hand and try to hold back the smile that is about to burst from my face. "Fair enough."

He shuts the door behind me and we walk to the front door. The crisp air cools the heat spreading across my cheeks like wildfire. I take a deep breath and look down at the cobblestone, catching a glimpse of Gabe's hand in mine. I pull it away and open the door before he can grab it.

Antonio greets us the second we walk inside. He holds up his hands to greet us the same way my aunt Lori does when we travel to her house for a holiday dinner. "You kids look great. You're going to love it here at Vesuvius."

I smile and nod.

Gabe holds out his hand to shake Antonio's. "I can't wait. After tasting your gingerbread creation I'm making sure I save room for dessert."

Antonio gives his hand a shake. He takes our coats and puts his hand in the small of my back almost pushing me further into the restaurant. "I have a wonderful table for you two kids."

My eyes sweep Gabe from head to toe. His perfectly tailored suit hugs his body, showing off a subtle view of the mountainous terrain of his muscles. Heat flashes through my body like Vesuvius itself just erupted. I walk slowly, like I'm on my way to the *Hotel California*, where I can never leave once I step in.

We make our way to the back of the restaurant. A table sits near a marble fireplace and a Christmas tree decorated with red, white, and green ornaments. The red napkins and dim lighting make it look like I'm on a romantic Christmas getaway in Italy.

God dammit, this is a date.

Antonio pulls out the chair for me and Gabe stands until I sit down. I look at the intricately set table. Great, now I have to try and remember what fork to use first. We probably could've discussed things over a pizza on the couch. I run through the scenario in my head for a minute. Yeah, being alone on a couch with Gabe is way more dangerous than this.

The waiter comes over and pours some water. I grab mine the second he's finished and slug it down like a college kid sucking down her first beer at a frat party.

Gabe scrunches his eyebrows and then turns toward the waiter. "Let's start with your best cabernet sauvignon."

"Coming right up sir." The waiter scurries away.

"Red wine pairs well with most Italian food. Are you a wine drinker or do you just mainline water?"

I finish the last drop in my glass and set it down on the table. "I like a nice glass of wine." Drinking it or throwing it, it never seems to fail.

I pull out a notepad from my purse. "Okay, I figure once we order we can start talking about what ideas you have for generating business at the farm."

He reaches over the table and places his hand on mine, covering the small notebook and pen. Chills sweep through me the second his skin touches mine. "How about we try a different approach?" He takes the notepad and pen out of my hand and puts it in the pocket of his suit jacket.

I nibble my lip and stare at the perfectly fitted fabric, clinging to every curve in his chest just the right way. My heart rate triples. "What do you have in mind?"

He unbuttons his suit jacket and takes it off, slinging it over his chair. The blue dress shirt underneath outlines his chiseled torso. I press my lips together, afraid of what might slip out if I release the pressure.

"Let's just relax, talk, and have a nice dinner. You can think of it as brainstorming." He looks around. "This isn't the kind of place where you take notes or pull out a PowerPoint presentation."

I take a breath and relax my muscles a bit. "Agreed."

The waiter returns with the bottle of wine in a chiller and the menus. "Our additional features for tonight are crab-stuffed lobster tail in hollandaise sauce and steak Diane for two, perfect for romantic couples like yourselves."

I cough and clear my throat. "Sorry."

"Thank you. We'll just need a few minutes."

"Steak Diane for two? What do you say, partner?" Gabe winks.

"Not partners, just two people helping each other out." I peruse the menu. Who am I kidding, the steak Diane is to die for. "Fine. Let's go for the steak."

He takes the bottle of wine from the chiller and pours us each a glass. "No reason to wait for the waiter to return."

I chug down the wine the second he stops pouring. Maybe a

little alcohol in my system can calm me down a bit. I set the glass down after gulping down half of the wine in it.

He swirls the wine in his glass and takes a deep breath before taking a sip. "Excellent."

Great, he's a wine connoisseur and I'm acting like a girl trying to get buzzed up in a parking lot before the big concert. I lean back in my chair and take a small sip. "Antonio has the best wines in town."

The waiter comes back over and Gabe orders the Steak Diane for two along with a bruschetta appetizer. Okay, time to put everything on the table.

"I think Antonio is on team Gabe, and you might have even converted Belle."

"Not a chance." He pours me another glass of wine. "I think I have a plan that everyone in town might like better than the original letter."

"A meteor coming down and swallowing our town is better than the original letter." I sip the fresh glass of wine. "What are you thinking?"

"The rate for anyone fixed would obviously stay the same. Most of the town went for the variable rate, which I have no idea why, and that rate would increase by one percent and then I'd lock it in for them. As for late fees, I will give a ten-day grace period. After that, it will be a thirty-five-dollar fee. If anyone is having a hard time, they can come see me and we will work it out. What do you think?" He nibbles his lip.

I nod. "Sounds pretty fair and I think everyone will probably go for it. It shows you care about the people and the town." I sit back as the waiter places the bruschetta in the middle of the table. "I can't guarantee they're going to trust you, though."

"I'm getting there. Especially since you're on team Gabe." He bites into the appetizer.

I take a piece of bruschetta. "Um. I'm on team Evergreen Falls." I take a bite. The flavors of fresh tomato, mozzarella, and balsamic vinegar flow through my taste buds. It's one of the best things I've ever tasted. "It looks like things are working out for you though. Now my turn."

He wipes his lips with his napkin. "Definitely. I'm a man of my word." He holds up a finger as he finishes chewing. "I've got a great plan. Evergreen Falls Winter Carnival held at the Watkin's Family Tree Farm."

I scrunch my eyebrows. "Sounds like a ridiculous amount of work."

"I told you. I've got that all covered. Here's a quick rundown. We set up booths, and we can just add to the ones already there from the Gingerbread Competition, charge vendors a small fee to rent one for the carnival, you charge an entrance fee."

I open my mouth to speak but he holds up his hands.

"Give me a chance."

I nod.

"Every entrance ticket gets the person a chance to win a big screen TV that will be raffled off at the end of the carnival. All the vendors keep the money they earn, you keep the money for renting the booths and the entrance fees. Savings and Loan will sponsor the event and also rent a booth. You've got everything to gain and nothing to lose."

I tap my fingers on the table, trying to find a loophole in his plan. It seems pretty solid. Jeez, maybe I should work on my trust issues. What the hell, he might have something here.

"Okay."

"Really, no argument?" His eyes widen.

"Sounds like something I'd like to try… I'm in." I hold out my glass.

He lifts his glass. "To the winter carnival."

We clink glasses and each take a sip.

Antonio comes over, a smile the size of a big pizza pie gracing his face. "You two kids remind me of me and my Maria when we were young."

There's no way I can explain to him this is just a business meeting and not a date so I flash a smile.

"Buon appetito," He places a plate in front of each of us.

I breathe in the aroma of the steak in a brandy cream sauce served with garlic mashed potatoes and broccoli. I'm fairly certain this dish was created in heaven.

"Antonio, this looks exquisite. Now that Nat is showing me the town, you'll definitely be seeing me around here more often." He holds out his hand and shakes Antonio's again.

"Hope to see both of you here." He winks at me and heads back to the kitchen.

Does Antonio think I'm sleeping with Gabe or something? Sorry, my heart belongs to the town but the rest of my body doesn't.

We cut into our perfectly cooked steaks and savor the culinary delight. I finish everything on my plate a few minutes after Gabe.

"Antonio could make an empire for himself in L.A."

"He's a talented chef, but once he moved here and opened up Vesuvius he fell in love with Evergreen Falls. He'd never leave even if it means he's holding himself back. He's happy and that's all that matters."

"True. Can't buy happiness." He sips the last bit of wine.

The waiter comes over. "Antonio has a special dessert for you two. His amore cannoli." He places a plate with four small cannoli in front of us, two red ones and two green ones.

"Thank you." Gabe stabs a green one. "Pistachio. It's like I've died and gone to heaven."

I stick my fork into a red one. Red velvet shell with ricotta filling and tiny chocolate morsels. "Gabe you've got to taste this. It's better than s—" I stop myself before I say sex and turn this business meeting from G to PG. I've got to change the subject, quick.

"I've got to string some lights on the tree for City Hall tomorrow morning and have Clyde deliver it."

"I haven't even lit up the beauty I grabbed at your tree farm yet."

"What?" I say louder than I should.

He shrugs. "My family are more New Year's people, remember. I am still getting settled in my house, but I haven't put a tree up since we had the artificial one in the family homestead. So it's been about eight years since I had a Christmas tree."

I grab my chest and bend forward like he just shot me in the heart.

"Yeah, I know. The second your tree made its way into my house, everything changed… got better, like my life since I met you."

I sit up and lay off the theatrics. "Thanks," I say, so quiet it's almost a whisper. Warmth flows through my body. It's been forever since someone said anything even remotely close to that to me. Who knows? That right there may be the best compliment of my life so far.

"Just saying it like it is."

The waiter comes over and sets the bill down in front of Gabe. I reach my hand for it but he snatches it away before I get the chance. "I'm assuming the risk and this is a business meeting, right?"

I'm not so sure. The whole night felt like a really good date. I nod and flash a smile while he stuffs the vinyl folder with cash and hands it to the waiter.

"Back to the City Hall tree lighting." He rubs his chin.

Yes, thank god, let's talk business. "What do you want to know?"

"Is there a special tree, like the New York one?"

"Even better. It's a tree from our farm. We pick out the tallest and fullest one and donate it to the town every year. It's a tradition."

He holds up a finger. "What do you think about shaking things up?"

I scrunch my forehead. "Not sure, what do you have in mind?"

"How about Evergreen Savings & Loan donates a tree from the Watkin's Family Tree Farm?"

Hmm. I'd have to run that one by Mom but she's currently obsessed with Gabe so I don't think it would be a problem.

"One more thing. I'll donate baked goods from Sugar Plum Bakery. Every person who stops by City Hall to admire the tree, or other business, gets a gourmet Christmas cookie, or whatever Belle wants to make."

"Now you're thinking like a small town businessman trying to win over the townspeople." I let out a chuckle. "You're scared to death of Belle, aren't you?"

"I leave my nightlight on every night, in case it's the night she's going to try to kill me."

We both laugh.

"I'll let Mayor Stevens know and I'll text Belle. You're giving her less than twenty-four hours notice on those cookies so I'd keep on two nightlights."

"Noted."

I stand up. "We should probably get going before Antonio starts singing us Italian love songs."

"I might want to stay for that." He winks and stands up, placing his hand in the small of my back to lead us to the door.

Antonio rushes over, grabbing our coats on the way. "Have a wonderful night you two and don't forget to come back again soon." He raises his eyebrows.

I'm not sure if he's a hopeless romantic but he needs to stop trying to play matchmaker. Gabe and I are working together, that's it.

Gabe holds my coat for me while I put in on. I'd normally take it from him and do it myself but gentleman are hard to come by these days. I button it up while Gabe slides his coat over his suit jacket. He waves to Antonio and holds open the door for me.

The crisp air sends my body into shivers. The temperature really dropped during our two-and-a-half-hour dinner. I fold my arms over my chest to keep warm.

Gabe puts his hands on my arms and moves them up and down creating warm friction.

My heart races. I should stop him, but I don't. Is it because it's been a while since I've been out with a guy? Maybe I'm afraid of hypothermia and it's not in my best interest to nip this in the bud. Mom and Antonio can't be right about us.

He guides me to his car. "I'll warm her up as soon as I can." He clicks the key fob and opens the passenger side door.

I sit inside and he closes the door, scurrying to the other side and firing up the engine. "Don't worry, the horses will do their thing with the motor and have heat on in no time." White water vapor forms with every breath he takes. He rubs his hands together. "I've got to remember to keep gloves in here." He fiddles in his center console. "Oh, before I forget. I need your expertise."

Right now my mind can't think of anything other than how sexy the white vapor coming off of his lips looks in the moonlight shining in through the windshield. "I'll try my best."

"I picked up some lights and a few ornaments from Evergreen Hardware for my tree. They're still sitting in the bag but since I'm a tree-lighting virgin, I have no clue the best way to string up the lights and decorate. Oh, and I bought a stand that fills with water. Not sure exactly how to set it all up."

The heat kicks in and the vapors disappear from his breath. "Wait, are you calling me a tree whore?" I hold in a smile.

"What?" He holds up his hands. "No, you're the queen of Evergreen Falls Christmas trees."

"I can live with that one." I let out the smile. "I'll give you a quick tutorial. Let me know when you're free and I'll stop by."

He looks at his wrist pretending to check a watch. "How

about right now? Unless you have other plans." He pulls out of the parking lot and heads onto the road.

Come on, Nat, think of something... anything to get out of this one. Early day tomorrow, my mother is afraid to stay at the farm herself, I turn into a werewolf in moonlight. Okay, all of those are terrible. I struggle to think of something that actually makes sense. The wine is clouding my judgment. I'm going with lots of work tomorrow. I open my mouth to speak, "Okay."

Dammit.

CHAPTER 5

TREE LIGHTING

THERE'S A CHRISTMAS TREE EMERGENCY AND I'M THE MOST qualified person to handle the situation. I try repeating that in my head until I actually believe it. How the hell did I get myself into this situation? Right, lack of coordination between my brain and my mouth. Sure, I can blame the wine but it's more than that. Why does Gabe have this unseen power over me that pretty much renders my brain useless?

Could Belle be right? Of course he's not Satan but maybe he's a playboy who knows exactly what to say and when to say it. I've only had two boyfriends and neither of them were the smoothest in the romance department. Maybe it's his L.A. charm. I've got to watch myself and keep it professional.

Plus, I don't want word getting around that I gave him a tree that lost all of its needles or died before Christmas. Talk spreads around the town like wildfire. I'll set up the tree, instruct him on how to care for it, and head home. It's a perfect plan.

Gabe turns the dial on the radio to the soft rock channel that plays Christmas music from Thanksgiving until New Years. "I thought I'd get us into the spirit."

"Sounds like a plan." *Jingle Bell Rock* blasts through the

speakers. I can't help smiling when Christmas music flows through the airwaves. It started when I was a little girl and we'd sit around the Christmas tree drinking mom's famous hot chocolate. Dad would turn up the Christmas tunes and we'd talk about our favorite traditions. Of course I was all about Santa but as I got older my favorite tradition was sitting there with my family. Every time *Jingle Bell Rock* played, Dad jumped up and pulled Mom off her chair. I hopped up and we would turn the living room into a dance party. I miss those times the most.

Gabe sways in his seat, almost like he's dancing to the beat. The song must have the same effect on everyone. I give in to the music and do a little dance of my own.

We continue down the road and turn off onto Willow Lane. Gabe bought Mr. Hooper's Victorian house in the deal with the Savings and Loan. I gaze up at the yellow and white home, complete with a turret and wrap-around porch. The moonlight along with the lampposts illuminate it just enough to see the intricate gingerbread woodcarvings.

Last time I was here was at a wedding for Mr. Hooper's daughter, Katie. The flowers and landscaping could have rivalled a celebrity event. Dozens of roses of every color and hydrangea bushes perfectly pruned. Once spring hits, Gabe is in for a spectacular display.

Plus, he could host his family and probably even his surfer friends. Five bedrooms and three baths, it would make an amazing Bed and Breakfast. Gabe must get lost in that house.

I know exactly where the tree should go. It should be centered in the turret where the five windows display the back and sides of the tree for the outside view. The front of the tree would face whatever furniture Gabe has in the room.

He pulls into the driveway. "You look like you're casing up the joint. Have you been here?"

I blink and pull myself out of my thoughts. "Yes. Mr. Hooper had some events here since the house and property are so big. It's amazing."

He nods. "Yeah, houses in L.A. like this one are hard to come by unless you're rich and famous. I'm still working on both those things." He winks.

He shuts down the engine and gets out, hopping over to my side to open the door for me. I take his hand and step outside. Why do I feel like a princess going to the ball?

Remember, Nat. You're here to work. "I know the perfect place to set up your tree." I gaze at the lit up turret. *Wait, what am I doing? Shouldn't he decide where things in his home should be placed?* "I mean, I have some suggestions."

He bites his lip. "You are the tree boss. Whatever you say goes." He walks toward the front door, gently pulling me with him.

I look down, realizing I'm still holding his hand. Okay, no need to panic. I will pull it away when he opens the door. We walk up the three steps to the front porch and he fiddles with his keys. I yank my hand away, a bit faster than I meant to, and fold my hands together around my coat.

He opens the door and gestures for me to go inside. "After you."

I step inside and gaze at the open two-story foyer with a mammoth chandelier hanging down. The intricately plastered ceilings, yellow walls, and white crown molding send me back in time. It looks exactly as I remember, minus the boxes against the back wall and the lack of any type of décor.

He closes the door behind us. "I'm still getting settled. Moving is never fun, especially halfway across the country."

I nod, even though I've only moved across the hall from one bedroom to another. We head into the living room. I peruse the beautiful chandelier sending rainbows of color against the yellow walls. The windows in the turret send the perfect amount of moonlight inside. To the left of the windows, the tree leans against the wall. A box filled with newly purchased lights and yellow and green round ornaments sits on the floor beside the tree, along with a tree stand, still in its original box.

Okay I have some work to do. I set my purse on the burgundy leather couch facing a huge television. A matching love seat is on the left wall and a reclining chair to the right. I close my eyes and picture sitting on the couch with a cup of cocoa looking over at the tree in the window, with a virtual yule log on the television and some Christmas music in the background.

"It's all yours." Gabe points at the tree and decorations.

He pulls me out of my trance. Yeah, none of this is mine and I'm getting way more involved than I should. He asked me to help him with the tree and that's what I'm doing. First time I'm setting up in a tree in a silky, black dress but I'm sure I can handle it.

"Can you grab a pitcher of water?" First step, make sure the tree survives.

He nods and heads off to the kitchen.

I walk over to the stand and break open the packaging, quickly assembling the few pieces and setting it down in front of the windows. I take a step back. Looks good here.

"Water." He sets a gallon of water down on the floor next to the box. "What can I do?" He smiles, his face almost lights up.

I can't help but follow suit. I guess it's his first time putting up a real Christmas tree. He should have the full experience. I walk over to my purse and take out my cell phone, clicking the Christmas channel on my satellite radio app. *Holly Jolly Christmas* blasts through the airwaves.

"The stand is ready. Let's set the tree inside and make sure it's anchored and we can add the water."

Gabe takes off his suit coat and slings it over the recliner. He hoists up the tree. The muscles in his arms dance as he carries the Douglas fir over to the stand. I try to breathe slow and deep to control my heartbeat.

He sets the stem of the tree into the stand. "Like this?"

"Yeah, I'll secure it with the pins." I kneel down and crawl over to the tree, centering the trunk and securing it to the stand. My dress creeps up with every move. I fling a hand back and try to pull it down so Gabe doesn't get a full view of my red underwear. Note to self, only wear jeans when setting up a tree.

I back up and roll to a sitting position. The Douglas fir is perfectly centered in the turret surrounded by windows. What a spectacular tree for his first one. "Looks good. Let's give him a little drink." I adjust my dress back to its former glory and pour the water into the stand.

"We need scissors to cut the rope around the tree." I always make sure I tie up the limbs whenever I'm selling a tree to prevent any breakage during travel.

Gabe almost skips to the kitchen and returns with a sharp knife. "Scissors are MIA, will this work?"

"Sure. You ready?" I take Gabe's arm. The second I touch him, tingles shoot through my body. Maybe I should ask myself that question.

I put my hand over his. The heat from his body makes my heart race. *Come on, Nat. Get it together, especially when there's a knife involved.* I try and steady my hand from trembling. "We're going to cut straight down here and the branches will spring open."

We slice the knife down the twine rope right to the bottom. The second the twine gives way and an array of branches pop out. One of the branches catches the bottom of my dress, pulling it up to my belly button. I gasp, and try my best to release the fabric, but the more I struggle the worse it is. I flail back and forth trying to do something... anything to save my dignity.

"Don't worry, I got it." Gabe slides the knife down to cut the branch.

The sound of ripping fabric rings in my ears. I look down at the slice Gabe makes in my dress. I step back and the fabric releases. A slit forms right down the front of my dress.

"Nat, I swear to God it was an accident." He drops the knife and holds up his hands.

I look down at my dress and then up at him.

We both look at each other and burst into laughter.

He drops his hands and shakes his head. "In my defense, I did say it's my first tree trimming."

I try and hold my dress together. "Very true."

He grabs his coat and hands it to me to tie around my waist. "I'm pretty sure we're not in the proper dress code."

I hang his coat in front of my dress. "Listen, I'm not ruining and wrinkling your suit jacket to cover up. I'll come back and we can do this another time when I'm... dressed more appropriately."

He holds up a finger. "I've got an idea." He rushes out of the room and stomps up the steps, returning a few seconds later with two oversized sweatshirts and drawstring shorts made out of the same material.

He hands one of each to me. "Girls loved wearing these...well not these, but shorts and shirts like these on the beach at night when it gets cooler."

I take the outfit. "Might as well bring a little L.A. to your first official Christmas tree."

He starts unbuttoning his shirt. I stare for a second and then instinctively turn around. Okay, this is taking a major turn. "Maybe we should finish up tomorrow."

"Sorry. When you're a surfer it's just habit." He moves around to face me, pulling on his sweatshirt. "Bathroom is the second door down the hall."

I take off down the hallway clinging to the clothes. Okay, nothing good can come out of this night. I head into the bathroom and close the door. It's one thing to help him with his tree but now that I'm half naked I think it's time to put this night to bed. I glance in the mirror at my tattered dress. Who the hell would think something like this could happen outside of a sitcom? I look up at the ceiling. "Thank you, universe. Funny."

Well, I can't have him take me home like this, so the surfer clothes are my only option. I change into the oversize sweatshirt and roll up the sleeves. The shorts are huge. I pull the drawstring tight and tie the same knot I use when I'm roping up a Christmas tree. Well, this is as good as it gets.

Since he won't take no for an answer, I'll trim the tree as fast as I can and head home... in the middle of the winter in shorts. Whatever. Maybe I should call Belle to bring me clothes. Dear God, what am I thinking? Besides the fact the whole town would know in ten minutes, she'd never believe the truth.

I sigh and head out of the bathroom, let's get this show on the road. I toss my torn dress in my purse.

"Looks great." His eyes sweep my body from my head to my toes.

Tingles sweep through me. "Thanks." The sweatshirt clings to his body with just enough tightness to show off glimpses of his chiseled torso.

"Okay, next up are the lights." I head over to the tree and make sure the branches are all released. No need for another mishap.

Gabe heads over to the box and takes out the lights. The shorts follow the curves in his tight butt. I try to look away but my eyes gravitate toward him. He's the perfect mix of brains and brawn. I'm in more trouble than I thought.

"Got the lights." He holds out the cord.

I take it and plug it in. "Drape them over the branches like this so they're secure." I weave the lights in between the small branches.

He comes up behind me and holds the string. "Like this?" He sandwiches me between the tree and his body while he drapes the lights on the branch. His warm breath on my neck sends shockwaves through my body.

"Yes," I say, my voice cracking.

My heart pounds in my chest. He tucks a few stray strands of hair behind my ear and reaches up to adjust the lights. I duck down under his arm and spin around in a move you'd see on a basketball court.

I take a few steps back. "Looks good so far."

He drops his arm and turns to me, and then moves back to look at the tree. "I'm getting the hang of this." He grabs another set of lights and plugs it into the outlet.

"Hang on." I walk over and unplug the set from the outlet. "They plug into each other." I reach for the end of the light set on the tree, standing on my tippy toes.

"I got it." He stands behind me and takes the cord, plugging in the new set. "Like this?"

His rock-hard body presses against me as he lights up the new set. "Ah ha." It's all I can get out. I make my move again and head to the middle of the room. "You've got it. I think you can finish up the lights."

There's no way I'm going back to string lights on the tree. If I'm in that situation one more time the universal force trying to pull us together might win. I take a deep breath. *Come on, Nat. You are hanging out with Gabe to work together, that's all. Mutual benefits for both parties.*

"Looks like that's all she wrote." He steps back and gazes at the multitude of white lights illuminating the tree.

"Now it's starting to look like a Christmas tree." I shift my gaze to the box of ornaments. Once those are on, we can stick on the star and I can head home, task accomplished.

Gabe bends over to get the ornaments from the box. My gaze shifts, pouring over his hot body like chocolate syrup on a sundae. My breathing increases. Dear God, I need to throw on these ornaments and get out of here. Note to self, no more wine when it's a day I'm working with Gabe.

I walk over to the ornaments and rip open the package of hooks. "No trick to this one. Just put them on wherever you like as the tree speaks to you." I take a green ornament and hook it up, placing it on the tree. The lights reflect off the glittery sphere.

Rockin' Around the Christmas Tree sounds through the room. Gabe hooks his ornament and dances around. I chuckle and sway to the music. He places a red ornament on a branch and turns toward me, grabbing my hands.

We dance together like junior high kids at the first school dance. The negative thoughts flow out of my brain with the music. He steps back and I spin around while he holds my hand. It's been forever since I danced alongside a Christmas tree. They lyrics pour from my mouth as I dance around with Gabe.

The song ends and we both stand, smiling at each other.

"If I knew putting up a Christmas tree would be this much fun I would've done it a long time ago." He grabs another ornament and puts it on the tree.

"Don't worry, you've got me to show you the ropes." Okay, that didn't come out right but he gets the point.

We finish trimming the tree until all the ornaments are on it. We both take a step back. It's perfect.

"All it needs is the star." Gabe takes the star from the box. "Will you do the honors?"

I peruse the treetop. Even though I've done this hundreds of times, I want to make sure this tree is perfect. "Of course, do you have a stepladder?"

"It's on my list of things to pick up." He rubs his chin. "I've got an idea. Do you trust me?"

Jury is still out on that one. "I think."

"Any chance you were a cheerleader?" He hands me the star.

"Sorry," I shake my head.

"We'll improvise." He moves behind me and puts his hands on my hips.

Shockwaves shoot through me like I was just electrified. He lifts me up to the top of the tree. I wobble for a minute before I get my bearings straight. Okay, this is one way to put up the star. His hands ride up underneath the hem of the oversized sweatshirt, coming in direct contact with my skin. My heart races the second his hands touch me. I force myself to breathe slow and steady. I've got get this star on the tree before I burst into flames. Gabe holds me strong and still. I reach up and bunch a few branches together, sticking the star onto them. I twist it to make sure it's secure and centered, then plug it into the light string. It shines bright, illuminating the room.

I move it a smidge and take another look. "It's perfect."

Gabe takes a step back to see the finished product. The second he moves I sway from side to side. I straighten my torso to and try to balance myself but my body has other ideas. Gabe loosens his grip a bit and I slide down, turning my body toward him on the way. I wrap my arms around his neck. He holds my waist tight. I slowly make my descent until my feet touch the floor. I can feel his heart beating against mine. The musky smell of his cologne sends a kaleidoscope of butterflies fluttering in my stomach. He moves his forehead against mine. My heart goes into overdrive. I stand frozen. He presses his lips against mine, soft at first and then slowly increasing in passion. I close my eyes and lose myself in Gabe's perfect kiss.

The doorbell rings. I pull away and gasp. Oh God, what the hell just happened?

Gabe drops his hands from my waist. "Who could that be? You're my only friend here."

Is that what we are? Who the hell knows anymore?

He blows out a breath with puffed cheeks. "Be right back." He heads to the door.

I've got to get out of here. I spot my shoes by the side of the couch. Once he takes care of his unexpected guest, I'm gone.

"Gabe, your place is cute." A woman clutching a Gucci bag walks in the foyer, looking the place up and down.

"Yeah, thanks. What are you doing here, Victoria?"

Oh god, is it an old girlfriend? Or maybe a current one. I fidget with my fingers.

"My flight got in later than I thought. I had to come see your new business endeavor and tell you the news in person. The job at Wallace in New York City came through and it's yours. You hit the big time. The best news is that you can keep this," she sways her arms around, "as a side project. Everybody wins."

So Gabe is jumping ship. I let out a low groan. Typical. What was he trying to prove with this falling-in-love-with-the-town, bullshit? Is seducing me a challenge he needed to conquer? Hate to tell him, but it's not going to happen.

She pulls out a bottle of champagne from her oversized bag. "I thought we'd have a drink and celebrate." Her heels click against the hardwood floors. She stops at the entrance to the living room. "Sorry, I didn't realize you had company."

I shake my head and hold up my hands. "Nope, just helping with the tree. In fact, I was just leaving." I slip on my shoes and grab my coat and purse from the couch.

"Natalie, this is Victoria, one of my business associates." Gabe introduces us.

I hold out my hand and shake hers. "Nice to meet you. I've really got to go."

"Wait, I'll drive you." Gabe lunges for his coat.

I shake my head. "Nope, I'm fine. See you at the carnival." I hightail it out the door and pull out my cell phone the second I round the corner.

Belle answers on the second ring. "What did he do?"

"Just come get me. I'm at Mr. Hooper's old place."

"On my way." She hangs up.

When besties were chosen, I got the greatest one in the world. I hold my coat around me, my legs shivering from the cool winter wind. A stray tear falls down my cheek. What the hell is wrong with me? We were only business associates, that's all, and from what Victoria said, he's keeping his business here too.

Another tear falls. Ugh, this is ridiculous. I'm crying over nothing. The Savings & Loan is back in the good graces of everyone in town. Everything we planned out has succeeded. The tree farm is getting much needed new business. He kept up his end of the bargain and so did I. It's over, the business agreement has been met.

He can go to New York City and be the exact man I thought he was before we spoke. Everything will be the same as it was before he got here.

Except it won't.

CHAPTER 6

WINTER CARNIVAL

TIME IS OF THE ESSENCE. I HAMMER A SMALL NAIL INTO THE STAND and string up a set of Christmas lights. Winter carnival is tonight and I've got to be ready. It's been almost a week and I managed to dodge every call and impromptu visit Gabe made to the tree farm. There's really no point, our work together is finished and after tonight he can head off to New York and probably hire some people to take care of business here. I let a sigh escape.

Belle plugs in the lights and leans against the stand. "I don't get it, why don't you just talk to surfer boy and quit all this moping around?"

I give her the side eye and continue stringing up the lights. "Have you been hitting the eggnog? I'm fine."

She rolls her eyes. "Please. I was ready to battle when I picked you up but he didn't do anything but offer you a ride and take some job in New York. Admit it, you're into him."

I step down from my chair ladder. "I helped him, he helped me, we're good." I set the hammer down on the stand. "Plus, he's not my type."

Belle squints her eyebrows. "Gorgeous, rich, funny, smart.

Yeah, every woman's nightmare." She takes a few steps back to examine her stand. "Why are you torturing yourself?"

"Okay drama llama." I attach some green and red garland to the side of the stand as a finishing touch.

Belle comes over and puts her hand on my shoulder. "Seriously. You haven't dated anyone since that jerk Les. Why?"

Maybe because I'm sick of feeling the way I do right now. It's ridiculous really. Gabe and I weren't even dating. I guess I just let my guard down for a minute but it's back up now. "I'm focusing on building up the farm, no time for anything else."

"That's bullshit."

Okay, how about because I see how life is for my mother after my dad passed. Sure she plasters on a smile and makes the best of things now, but I hear her cry herself to sleep some nights. The glow that lit up the room faded.

"I haven't seen you smile the way you did at the Gingerbread Competition in years. Maybe you should give surfer boy a chance."

"Sorry, not interested. And since when did you join team Satan?"

"I may have overreacted with the whole Satan deal. And I'm on team Natalie, maybe you should join us."

I roll my eyes. "The place looks great, I think we're ready for tonight. See you later." I grab my tools and head over to the house.

Ditching Belle isn't the classiest move, but I need to get away. I don't want to talk about why I'm not throwing myself at Gabe or anyone else in town. There're worse things than being alone, like being hurt. I'm an independent woman and can handle things myself, just like I've always done.

I head into the house and set the tools back in the toolbox. The scent of chocolate chip cookies flows through the air. Mom probably made five hundred of them for the carnival tonight. She sits at the kitchen table reading a book and sipping tea.

I take off my coat and pour a cup for myself. "We're set for tonight."

She puts her book down and gestures for me to join her. "Have you talked to Gabe?"

I shake my head no. "No reason to, everything is ready."

She presses her lips together and then releases them. "Did you guys have a fight or are you still embarrassed about the Christmas-tree-dress-ripping incident?"

I roll my eyes. "No to both questions." I sip my tea.

She puts her hand on mine. "What's going on, Natalie?"

"Nothing."

She huffs. "Please, you were so happy spending time with Gabe and now all of a sudden you're avoiding him like the plague. I thought you'd finally found somebody. That's all I want for you, honey."

I shake my head. "Mom, I can survive just fine without a man and he's leaving anyway for a big position in New York city. We were only business associates anyway and everything is taken care of so our working together is over."

She finishes her tea. "I've seen you two together and you were more than business associates, even if you won't admit it." She gets up from the table. "He called for you twice today, maybe you should talk to him."

I take another sip of tea. "I'll see him tonight." I slide her book over to check out what she's reading. *Love is all You Need.*

"Really Mom, this is what you're reading?" I hold up the book.

She snatches it out of my hand. "Nothing better in life than a great romance, I wish you'd realize that." She takes off and slides into the recliner in the living room with her book.

Belle comes into the kitchen. "Debbie Downer, you still got your panties in a bunch?"

"Yep, she does." Mom yells from the living room.

I jump up from my chair. "God, you two are relentless." I throw my hands in the air. "Don't you get it? He's leaving."

58

Belle walks up to the table. "And what if he wasn't? Then what?"

I shrug my shoulders. "Guess we'll never know."

"For someone who's already got one foot out of the door, he's trying like hell to talk to you or see you with all these visits and phone calls," Mom yells from the other room.

"Yeah, 'cause we have this carnival going on." I take a calming breath.

Belle shakes her head. "Sorry to break it to you, but it's a hell of a lot more than that. Everyone can see it but you."

I huff. "I don't even know why I bother talking to you two. That romance novel you're reading," I point toward Mom's book, "is purely fiction and it's not what's going on here, so stop trying to turn my life into your fantasy." I head through the hallway and up the steps to my room, away from this conversation.

It's Beginning to Look a Lot Like Christmas blasts through the outdoor speakers. We lucked out for the carnival, it's a clear night, around forty-five degrees and just a light breeze. I breathe in the fresh air and slowly exhale, trying to rid myself of the negative energy inside. I barely spoke to Gabe since the tree-lighting incident. Out of sight and out of mind, right? Except that he managed to etch himself on my brain no matter how hard I tried to prevent it from happening. I'll never admit to Belle or my mom, though. Doesn't matter. He's leaving and that's the end of it. It's not like he vowed to stay here, but if that was the case, why did he put so much work into winning over the townspeople?

I didn't help with the carnival much other than setting up our booth, but he said from the start of this winter carnival project he was going to take care of everything, and boy did he deliver. I look around at the multitude of lights strung from all areas of the farm. The Christmas music streams from the new PA system he had installed, a corral of real reindeer is stationed right before the rows of Christmas trees for sale, Santa sits in a huge red rocking chair with the Watkin's Tree Farm logo on top, and horse-drawn carriage rides run through the rows of evergreen trees still growing for next season's harvest. Santa's workshop has nothing on this place.

"Hey stranger, what do you think?" Gabe sneaks up next to me, holding out a bouquet of white poinsettias, the edges of their petals dipped in silver and gold glitter.

A smile escapes from my face. Dammit, he's breaking me down. How the hell am I going to turn him into a casual acquaintance after spending so much time together so far? The only way to stop whatever was starting between us is to stay away from him, just like I've been doing. I can't be rude either, though. I take the flowers. "You nailed it, just like you said you would."

"Santa's been easier to reach than you, the last week. What's going on?" He scrunches his eyebrows.

I start talking really fast and moving my hands around like I'm about to land a plane. "You know it's right before Christmas. One of the busiest times here at the farm and I was helping Belle with her booth and all her orders. Then I had to decorate, and Mom and I made cookies. Not a free moment." I crack him in the face with a poinsettia while talking with my hands.

Real smooth, Nat. "Oh my God, I'm so sorry."

Glitter flies into his hair. He blows air up toward his forehead, sending strands of his hair to and fro. "No biggie. Now I'm a little more festive."

"Hey guys, let me get a picture for the newspaper." Sam Grant, our local news reporter, points his camera at us.

Gabe throws an arm around me and sports his million-dollar smile.

Heat flows through me the second he touches me. I swallow hard and plaster on a smile. My only hope to survive this night is to get as far away from him as I can. The second Sam presses the shutter on his camera, I blurt out the first thing that comes to my mind. "Someone's got to man the booth. Catch you later Gabe." I take a few steps away from him, walking backwards. "Great job and an even better turnout." I gesture toward the line of people waiting to get in, and dart forward to make my escape.

Mom blocks my way. "I've got the booth, dear." She points toward the horse and carriage. "You two should take a ride. Great publicity for both of us." She winks.

I grit my teeth and shoot the glare of hellfire in her direction.

"Let me snap one more picture" Sam says.

Mom just about pushes me toward the carriage.

"Sure thing." I flash another smile at Sam and head toward the carriage, quickly jumping in. If the tree farm doesn't work out, maybe I can give acting a try.

"Thank you so much, Sam. Enjoy yourself and Merry Christmas." Gabe jumps into the carriage.

I smile for the picture talking through my teeth. "You know it's a picture, not a newscast, right? You sound like a politician."

"Who knows, maybe I'll run for mayor."

I roll my eyes. Yeah, I'm pretty sure the mayor can't live in New York and have town meetings through Zoom. I open my mouth to speak but quickly shut it. It's not worth the aggravation. Once this ride is over I'll take off to the booth, throw my mom out, and send her on a carriage ride with the most putrid single guy I can find.

Sam takes the picture a split second before the driver snaps the reins and the horse takes off. The force throws me a bit, knocking me right against Gabe. I squirm away. "Sorry."

"No complaints, here." He winks. "I've finally got a few minutes with you. Did you get my new letter?" Gabe nibbles his lip.

Oh yeah, I completely forgot. He sent all of his clients a new letter with the new terms. "I did, I think it's great. Anyone breaking down the doors to attack you?"

He shakes his head. "Nope. I was hoping you'd come by."

"Why? There's nothing left to do in the Gabe and Natalie business venture." I fidget with my fingers.

He puts his hand over mine. "I wanted to see you."

Electric shocks shoot through me. I pull my hand away.

He sighs. "Did I do something? You know, besides ruining your dress. You ran out of my place last week like a guy with a chainsaw was chasing you out of a haunted house." He tips up my chin. "I've already got you a gift card from the Evergreen Mall for a new dress."

I close my eyes and take a deep breath, trying to settle my nerves. I open them and flash a smile. "Nah, we're good. You did everything you wanted to. Goal accomplished. Go Gabe." I hold my hands up like I'm shaking pom-poms. Heat flashes across my face. Why am I so awkward when I'm a nervous wreck?

"Thanks. I don't want to lose my cheerleader though. What's going on?"

"You'll have a ton of cheerleaders in New York, maybe a whole cheering section." I fidget with my fingers. "Good luck, I know you'll do great."

He takes a breath and blows it out through puffed cheeks.

You know what, I don't want to hear about how it's such a great opportunity and everything he worked so hard to achieve. I'm really happy for him and he deserves all the success. I get it but it doesn't make me feel any better about being left behind.

I stand up.

The driver pulls on the reins. "Are you okay?"

Not even close. "I have to go, I'll see you both later." I jump off the side of the carriage into the farm.

"Nat, wait." Gabe hops off the carriage to follow me.

I duck through the Douglas Fir section that Dad and I planted a few years ago, and lose him within a few seconds. He calls my name about twenty times, the sound getting fainter the further I make it away from him.

CHAPTER 7

CHRISTMAS EVE

BELLE SLIDES THE SUNDAY EVERGREEN TIMES ON THE TABLE IN front of me. Smack dab on the cover is the picture of Gabe and I in the carriage. I scan the black and white photo and try and fight the smile threatening to escape. Gabe and I sit together, our faces aglow, like we're the homecoming king and queen. Even when I'm dressed to the nines, I've never seen myself look better. Is this what I look like when Gabe and I are together?

"Nice. The front page will give us great publicity." I dip my ricotta cookie into the icing glaze and shake on a few red and green sprinkles.

Mom mixes her chocolate chip cookie dough. "There's much more to that picture."

Belle takes a batch of cookies out of the oven and sets them on the cooling rack. "Come on, Nat. You like him."

I shrug my shoulders. "Everyone likes him, he's a nice guy." I dip another cookie in the icing.

"Why can't you just admit you're in love with him?" Belle raises her eyebrows.

I wipe the icing off my hands with a paper towel. "Have you gone crazy?"

"Nat, honey. I see it too. And that boy feels the same way about you. His face lights up like a Christmas tree every time you're anywhere near him." Mom adds some chocolate chips to the batter, a smile gracing her face.

"You've both turned insane. I'm going to have to send you to the psychiatric hospital for Christmas. We just worked on a project together, that's all. It's over and he's leaving anyway." I throw my arms in the air.

"Lots of great love stories start out by working together. Look at me and Clyde."

Okay, fine. Clyde and Belle met here when Belle was making baked goods to sell at the farm and Clyde bought just about every one she made. "It's not even close to the same."

"Sure it is."

"No... it's not. Clyde didn't make you fall for him and think you're finally going to get your happily ever after and then just leave you in the dust," I yell. I put my hand to my mouth. Did I just say that out loud?

Belle comes over and slides her arm around me.

Mom finishes the chocolate chip cookie batter. "Why don't you give him a reason to stay?"

I shake my head. "Let's just finish our girls' Christmas Eve cookie making tradition and forget this conversation ever happened. Besides, we have to get the pasta and fish dishes ready for Christmas Eve dinner once we finish our cookies." A stray tear rolls down my cheek. I wipe it up as quick as I can but Mom sees it.

"Look at you, you're giving up." She holds out a hand toward me. "Watkins women fight for everything they want, especially love." She comes over and puts an arm around me. "Did I ever tell you about the huge fight your dad and I had one Christmas Eve?"

"No. You guys were perfect, you never fought."

She drops her arm and sits on one of the stools near the island. "Oh honey, everyone argues sometimes. It's how you make up that counts." She sips a glass of water. "We were just engaged and had plans to get married and move out of Evergreen Falls to Boston."

"What?" Belle and I both yelled in unison.

Mom nodded. "That's right, we were going to get out of here and take over the world. Dad got a job at a big accounting firm and I had been accepted to Boston College to pursue a finance degree." She takes another sip of water. "The year before we got married, your Dad took me for a ride on Christmas Eve. He made me close my eyes the whole way. He pulled up to this piece of land with a large farmhouse on it and parked the car. When I got out and looked at it, I said 'That's nice,' and got back in the car. He was so nervous. I couldn't figure out why, he had already proposed and I had already accepted." She grabs a cookie and takes a bite.

Mom wanted to move out of Evergreen Falls for city life? I sit in the stool next to her. It's like my whole image of our lives has been changed.

"He handed me a gift-wrapped box. I smiled and ripped opened the red paper. Inside it was a deed to the property. I looked at him like he had ten heads. He took a deep breath and told me he didn't take the job in Boston and bought this land to start a Christmas tree farm. Once I figured out he wasn't joking, I stormed out of the car, tears running down my cheeks and walked down the road in my heels. He followed me, telling me how great our life was going to be, and that we weren't meant to be city folks. I ripped off the ring and gave it back to him."

Belle gasped. "You were going to call off the wedding?"

Mom nods. "Yep. I wanted to conquer the world. He chased me for forty-five minutes. I was at the point that I couldn't walk in my heels anymore. He stood in front of me with the ring in his hand. I had no choice but to listen to him. He said, 'Carol I love you more than life itself and I know we wouldn't be the people we are in Boston. We're meant to thrive here in Evergreen Falls.

I'll follow you to the ends of the earth but I know this is right. Will you give it a chance? Just for a year. If it doesn't work out, we'll go to Boston. Will you give it one chance?'"

She sips her water. "I'm not sure if it was the exhaustion or the look of love in his eyes that made me say yes. He carried me back to the property for the whole forty-five minute walk and took me up to the farmhouse. He opened the door, and out jumped a Golden Retriever puppy with a big red bow on its collar. That's the moment I knew I was home. He fought for me and gave me a reason to stay. I hope you can do the same with Gabe."

A tear rolls down my cheek. I look over at Belle and tears stream down her face too.

"Mom, that's the most romantic story I've ever heard."

Belle comes over to me and nudges my shoulder. "What are you still doing here?"

I shrug my shoulder. "Huh?"

"Nat, that boy is home all alone on Christmas Eve wondering why you won't even talk to him. No one should be alone at Christmas. If you really care about him, you'll fight." Mom puts her car keys on the newspaper. "Why are you still here?"

I look at the two of them and don't even think twice. I grab the newspaper, the bag of cookies I left on the counter, and my car keys, and head out the door.

I PULL UP TO THE VICTORIAN HOME. SUNLIGHT GLEAMS DOWN, reflecting sparkles on the light coating of snow. It illuminates the house, showing off its splendor. The Christmas tree we decorated together shines bright in the front window like it's a showcased piece of art. Gabe has it lit up even though it's only 3pm. The scene could grace the front of a Christmas card.

I park the car and take a deep breath, slowly exhaling. Gabe has never experienced a traditional family Christmas celebration and a few hours ago I was going to let him spend it alone. The Grinch has nothing on me. Mom and Belle were right, and thank god they talked some sense into me before it was too late. He should be with us for the holiday. No matter what happens, at least Gabe will have an Evergreen Falls-worthy Christmas.

I glance in the rear-view mirror and cover my mouth with my hand, then slowly drop it. Jeez, they could've told me I look like I've just emerged from a tornado. I run my fingers through my hair, trying to make myself semi-presentable. I fiddle with a few locks of hair. Well, that's as good as it gets. I open the door and step out of the car, giving my jeans a quick pat-down to get rid of the remnants of flour. On the plus, maybe I'll smell like fresh-baked cookies.

I head over to the passenger side and grab the bag and news-paper. The cool breeze flows through the air, caressing my face. I close my eyes and take a deep breath. I could wait forever and it wouldn't be enough time to calm my nerves. Okay, it's now or never. I've got to fix things between us.

I march up the sidewalk like a woman on a mission. The Christmas tree in the window looks so inviting. I move forward on the lightly snow-covered sidewalk as if I'm a moth to a light. My heart-rate triples. I walk up onto the front porch and lift my hand to ring the doorbell. Oh my God, what if Victoria is here? I stop dead in my tracks. I'm practically barging in on Gabe without even calling. What if he has plans or if he's not alone? A chill runs down my spine. I turn to go back to the car. I get one foot onto a step the second the door opens.

"Natalie?" Gabe's voice floats through the air. Tingles run through my body, just like they do every time he says my name.

I stop and turn toward him. "Hey, I was…" Okay, enough with the polite small talk. The whole *I was just in the area* isn't going to cut it. I mean, Evergreen Falls is a small town, I'm always in the area. Time to put the cards down on the table.

"I came here to see you." My voice crackles.

He stands in the doorway, leaning against the doorjamb. A red sweater clings to his body in just the right way, and those perfectly tailored black pants finish the look. Dear God, he could be the picture inside of one of those Christmas frames you see for sale on the store shelves.

"I'm glad you did." He steps to the side. "Come on in."

My heart races. It takes every ounce of energy to prevent myself from tackling him to the ground. I fidget with my fingers and follow him inside. The sound of Christmas music fills the space and the aroma of turkey invigorates my senses. Oh God, he's hosting. I need to go.

I take a step back. "I'm sorry, you're probably expecting guests. I should've called first. We'll talk later." I turn to dash back out the door, but Gabe grabs my free hand.

"I'm all by my lonesome and I've got all the time in the world." He takes a few steps toward me and moves his hand to the small of my back. "I wanted to take your advice, you know, since you're the Queen of Christmas, and have a traditional holiday the best I can." He gestures toward the kitchen. "I've got more turkey TV dinners if you're up for it."

I turn toward him so we're facing each other. "You got all dressed up and made a TV dinner for yourself?" I frown. Now I feel a million times worse. God, I suck.

He flashes a smile. "Yeah. And I have the music playing and tree all lit up. Best holiday I had in years… but now it just got better."

Heat rushes across my cheeks.

He looks at my hand holding the paper bag and newspaper. "No way, we made the front page?"

I hand him the paper and the bag. "Yeah, great publicity for both of us." What am I saying? It's like I'm still trying to convince myself we're only business associates. He means so much more to me.

He digs in the bag and pulls out three chocolate chip cookies and an ornament. I scrunch my forehead for a few seconds before it hits me. I was shopping at Jesse's General Store last week when I came across the ornament. I knew it was perfect for Gabe, but how did it get it there? Either mom found it, or I've got a guardian angel. Lightness fills my chest.

He holds up the ornament of a surfing Santa. "It couldn't be more perfect."

Yeah, no truer words have ever been spoken about the man in front of me. I take a few steps forward and back Gabe up into the archway of the living room. Okay, Nat. It's now or never. I wrap my arms around his neck and press my lips to his. My heart pounds and electric shocks flow through me. I pull away, sucking on his bottom lip.

He locks eyes with me, searching my face for answers.

I point up at the mistletoe. *Come on, Nat. No more excuses.* "Gabe, I've fallen for you." I take a deep breath. "And I don't know if you feel the same way but if you do, we can make it work. I know you've landed your dream job in New York, but people do things like this every day." Oh God, here I go, rambling on when I'm a nervous wreck. "I don't want to lose you."

He smacks his lips against mine, mid-sentence and then slowly pulls away. "I'm not going to New York. I came here because I wanted something different and I've found what I'm looking for. Plus Evergreen Falls has things New York doesn't."

I lower my eyebrows. "Really, like what?"

He presses his forehead against mine. "You."

I slide my hands to his cheeks and press my lips to his, unleashing the most passionate kiss I could ever dream up. We kiss under the mistletoe until the timer chimes.

"Dinner's ready, care to join me?"

"There's nowhere else I'd rather be." I take his hand and we both walk into the kitchen. "Prepare yourself for a colossal feast later on, more cookies than you've ever seen."

Gabe lets out a low groan. "Those cookies should come with a warning label, very addictive."

"Someone else should come with that label, too." I nuzzle into his shoulder. "Oh, and pack a bag because we all sleep over, get a little tipsy on egg nog, and wait for Santa."

He holds both of my hands. "On one condition."

I flash a smile. "Name it."

"There's got to be mistletoe." We kiss once more.

PLEASE REVIEW

We hope you enjoyed *Falling for Christmas* by Amy L. Gale. If you did, we would ask that you please rate and review this title. Every review helps our authors.

Rate and Review: Falling For Christmas

MEET THE AUTHOR

USA Today Bestselling author Amy L Gale is a romance author by night, pharmacist by day, who loves rock music and the feel of sand between her toes. She's the author of USA Today Bestsellers *Resisting Darkness* and *Resisting Moonlight;* Amazon New Adult Bestsellers, *Blissful Tragedy and Blissful Valentine,* along with *Christmas Blitz, Blissful Disaster, Bear Creek Cowboys: Bear Creek Rodeo series, Mine Before Midnight, Pull Me Under, and Fight For It.* When she's not writing, she enjoys baking, scary movies, rock concerts, and reading books at the beach. She lives in the lush forest of northeastern Pennsylvania with her husband, daughter, five cats, and golden retriever, Sadie. You can find her at

Read More from Amy L. Gale www.authoramygale.com